MW00479149

LOST FOR
CHRISTMAS

LOST FOR
CHRISTMAS

By Ted and Shirlene Hindmarsh

Horizon Publishers
Springville, Utah

ISBN-13: 987-0-88290-823-6

Published by Horizon Publishers, an imprint of Cedar Fort, Inc., 2373 W. 700 S., Springville, UT, 84663
Distributed by Cedar Fort, Inc., www.cedarfort.com

LIBRARY OF CONGRESS CATALOGING-IN-PUBLICATION DATA

Hindmarsh, Ted C.
  Lost for Christmas / Ted and Shirlene Hindmarsh.
    p. cm.
  ISBN-13: 978-0-88290-823-6 (acid-free paper)
  1. Christmas stories. I. Hindmarsh, Shirlene. II. Title.
  PS3558.I4775D86 2007
  813'.54—dc22

                    2007013369

Cover design by Nicole Williams
Cover design © 2007 by Lyle Mortimer
Edited and typeset by Erin L. Seaward

Printed in the United States of America

10 9 8 7 6 5 4 3 2 1

Printed on acid-free paper

WE'RE DELIGHTED THIS CHRISTMAS to present our first collaborative publication effort—a story that we hope illustrates the value of determination, love, faith, and prayer, and their roles in accomplishing the small, daily miracles that make life worth living.

We dedicate this work to our loved ones, who not only humor our eccentricities but also have provided the inspiration for this tale.

Best wishes and Merry Christmas!

—TED AND SHIRLENE HINDMARSH

CHAPTER ONE

BURT WATKINS EARNS HIS LIVING selling insurance. His wife, Sally, earns her living too, being a wife to her husband and a mother to five children. There is Courtney, who is sixteen; the twins, Denny and Danny, who are fourteen; Hailey, who is twelve; and Duncan (fondly known as "Dinkin" by his older siblings, for reasons that should become clear as this tale unfolds) who has just recently turned eight.

It should be known that this family is a well-behaved bunch (sort of), they like each other (for the most part), and they enjoy being together (occasionally). But they do have their moments. In short, they're normal kids. They tease, they play jokes on each other, and they generally have trouble settling down.

For the Watkins family, Christmas is big. Their presents are usually simple and few in number, but resourceful Mom and congenial Dad always make up for that by making sure the season is filled with traditions, good food, and fun.

This year, as a special Christmas treat, the Watkins family was setting out for an adventure—that is, if they could ever get everyone organized. They would be traveling six hundred miles to Aunt Millie's house for Christmas and for a long-overdue family vacation. They were all excited to see their relatives again, but they were not thrilled with the fact that they would be driving. Burt makes a fairly decent living, but with a large family, flying—especially at Christmastime—is out of the question.

The Watkins family lives in a huge metropolitan area on the west coast, and they had to travel inland to get to Carver City, which is Burt and Sally's pleasant, almost rural hometown. But to get there, they had to travel across hundreds of miles of some pretty desolate countryside. They had taken the trip several times before, and they did not particularly enjoy it.

This year, however, the saving grace was their mode of transportation: a huge motor home that Burt's boss offered for the occasion. He said he didn't use it that much, and he was very willing to lend it to them.

"You're welcome to it," he had said. "It's big and comfortable, and it can pass anything but a gas station. The only time you won't like it is when you fill it up, but it is still cheaper than flying. Plus, when you get there, you'll all have a comfortable place to sleep without overwhelming Aunt Millie's house."

Well, you can let your imagination run wild when you think of what it took to get that brood aboard— and most of it would be true. For example, Courtney needed her hair dryer, a complete makeup kit, and three large suitcases full of necessities; the twins needed their X-Box; and Duncan wouldn't go any- where without Bagley, his ridiculously large stuffed bear, without whom it was impossible for Duncan to go to sleep. But at last, and only three hours later than planned, everyone was finally loaded up, and the fam- ily was on their way.

For the most part, they fell in love with the motor home. It was almost as large as a passenger bus. In fact, they dubbed it the *Greyhound*. They knew this was going to be an all-night ride, and Burt, realizing what lay ahead, was grateful for the three-hour nap he took while the others were packing. Everyone found a favorite spot on the *Greyhound* except Duncan; he was all over the place. He finally settled in the back in a top bunk bed that nobody else wanted. He and Bagley, who is the source of a lot of teasing for Duncan, could curl up and avoid the taunts of the siblings.

After six long hours of travel, the huge gas tanks of the *Greyhound* were running low. The family's usual rest and gas-up stop on this trip was the Dogwood Creek Café and Truck Stop, an oasis of light and warmth right in the very middle of nowhere. As they pulled in, the blue numbers of the digital clock on the massive dashboard showed 1:03 a.m.

Everyone but Burt and Sally was soundly sleeping, and even Sally had been nodding in and out of consciousness. By now, Burt was really glad he had that nap.

As he pulled alongside a gas pump in the well-lit service bay, he announced loudly to anyone who cared to hear that this would be the last chance for a leg stretch and a store-bought goody before they reached Aunt Millie's.

Now, it should also be known that "store-bought goodies" were usually a no-no for this practical family of seven. Sally always kept an ample stock of carrots, celery sticks, and apples on hand for munchies, but she usually made a parental compromise on long road trips to entice good behavior from her children.

So far, everyone had been pretty good, so now it was time for Mom and Dad to pay up. The incentive was enough to arouse even the most sound sleeper. They all knew this was the one and only time Dad would be buying on this trip.

"If you don't get it now, don't grouse about it later," he bellowed good-naturedly.

As Burt inserted the nozzle of the gas hose into the gaping maw of the first of the *Greyhound's* two huge fuel tank fill pipes, he stretched his tense back and neck muscles and wondered audibly if they should have made the sacrifice and bought plane tickets. He set the automatic lock on the nozzle and grinned with amusement as he followed his sleepy pajama- and robe-clad brood as they stumbled one by one out of their comfortable sleep and into the small but cheery convenience store.

As usual, Duncan was the last one to get off. He was a very bright kid, but he was unpredictable. He often went off and did his own thing. One day, he was several hours late getting home from school. When his parents found him, he was sitting on the ground, looking down a small hole. He said he had followed a bug home and was watching to see what it was going to do next. Sometimes they wanted to get mad at him, but he was so likeable that it was hard to. Everyone took to him instantly, and, as a result, he usually got his way. But it bugged his parents that any time they wanted him to do something, he always had to do something else first.

Duncan pulled on his fuzzy slippers, but when he couldn't find his robe, he wrapped his favorite cuddly blanket around himself. Then he tucked Bagley into a large lump in the middle of the remaining covers.

"You keep the bed warm, Bags," he whispered into a barely visible, overstuffed ear. "I'll be right back with some corn chips and a drink."

As usual, Duncan was the first to place an order. Since any brand of corn chips and any kind of fizzy drink were his favorite "store-bought goodies," he never had to waste time making up his mind.

Burt made the purchase, handed Duncan the goods, and said, "Now don't go wandering, kiddo. Turn right around and get back on the *Greyhound*. You look dorky all wadded up in that blanket."

Duncan was usually pretty obedient—unless a better opportunity popped up along the way—and this time, as he passed under the arrow-shaped Restrooms sign, one did. Suddenly, he realized that he "had to go really bad." He almost always put it that way, because he almost never thought about it until it was suddenly a national emergency. There was a small lavatory on the *Greyhound*, but his sisters usually had that occupied. Besides, it was cramped and smelled funny, and the toilet made an irritating noise when you flushed it.

So without fanfare or anyone noticing, Duncan made what he was sure would be a quick pit stop.

"Getting these kids to move as a unit is like trying to herd cats," Burt quipped to the clerk as he paid the bill. Then he and Sally positioned themselves on either side of the ragged line of sleepy goody-munchers and prodded them back into the motor home.

Looking around with a practiced motherly glance, Sally said, "Where's Duncan?"

"Oh, you know him," Burt said. "He was the first one in line, so I fixed him up and sent him back on board."

When everyone was finally settled in for the final push, Burt turned in his pilot chair at the helm and called for a head count. Courtney, being the oldest and, by her own estimation, the most reliable of the offspring, made the count of her sleepy siblings, most of whom had gulped their goodies and were already back to sleep.

"Did Duncan make it?" Sally asked with motherly persistence. Courtney glanced up into the shadows of the topmost bunk bed in the back, and, sure enough, there was the expected pile of bedding with only the familiar ear of a big, stuffed bear visible.

"Yep, he's here. We're all present and accounted for," she reported.

"Okay, batten down the hatches," Burt yelled. "Next stop: Aunt Millie's!" And the *Greyhound* roared to life and turned back toward the freeway.

CHAPTER TWO

THE SMALL FOUR-ROOM COUNTY Sheriff's office in Millville, the county seat, was unpretentious and cluttered with maps and other official-looking documents. It barely had room for desks for the sheriff, his two deputies, and Maggie, the volunteer part-time dispatcher, who worked the late shift. But it still had the look and feel of an efficient rural law enforcement agency.

It was getting dark. Sheriff Rick Bennett was working late, as he usually did lately, and was just returning from a run out to the State University Extension Ranch to check on a report of vandalism to a tractor. He shut the door quickly, but the blowing snow swirled in anyway.

"Man, it's getting cold out there," he said as he shook off his hat before hanging it on a nearby peg. "The road crews were just alerted on the radio that a big one is blowing in. They're expecting up to a foot of snow on the valley floors."

"I'm glad you're back," Maggie said. "Rob Haskell from the Highway Patrol is waiting on line two. Can you talk to him?"

The sheriff grinned like he knew what was coming and sat down at his desk.

He punched the blinking red button and lifted the receiver to his ear. "How's traffic, Robert?" he bantered. "Keep your seat belt tight. I hear a big storm's blowin' in."

"Working late again, huh?" said the friendly voice on the other end. "We're going to have to raise a few taxes to get you some help, good buddy. It would be nice if you could go home once in a while."

"I appreciate your concern," the sheriff said, "but Maggie and I are keeping the peace, ain't we, Mag?" He grinned at Maggie's lifted eyebrows. "What can we do for the state troopers tonight?"

"This isn't official business, Rick," the trooper said. "Angie told Bess that you two didn't have anything planned for tomorrow night, and we just wanted to invite you over to spend it with us and the gang."

"Thanks for the offer, pal," the sheriff said, "but I've got a lot of work to catch up on. Angie said she might go over to the church Christmas party, but I think she'd just as soon sit home and watch a mushy video."

"Well, if you change your mind, you have a standing invitation," Rob said. He didn't want it to show, but his voice reflected a note of concern. Everybody knew that things were not going well between Rick and Angie, but nobody knew what to do about it.

"Hey, I'm glad you called, though," the sheriff said. "I just came through the stock underpass out by the Cedar Springs rest stop on my way back from the extension ranch, and there's a set of big tire tracks that loop down off the freeway, then back up onto it again. Whoever made 'em took out about thirty feet of fence. It looks like somebody fell asleep in a semi. Have you heard anything?"

"Nope, not a thing," Rob said. "Sounds like somebody got lucky, thank goodness. Whoever it is is counting his blessings right now. He's not likely to tell us anything. He knows what we'd have to say about it. But thanks for the tip. I'll call it in and get somebody on it right away before some animals wander through the hole and cause some real trouble. And Rick, think about that invitation. Getting out of the house together would do both you and Angie some good."

"Thanks, pal. I'll think about it, but don't wait up for us."

Trooper Stan Talbot, who had just joined the Highway Patrol after ending a career as a licensed therapist and who had only met both Rob and the sheriff a few months ago, overheard the conversation.

He had heard the rumors about the Bennetts' difficulties, but he didn't know the details.

"Nice try, Rob. Too bad he didn't take you up on your offer," Stan said.

"Oh, he never does," Rob said. "But I'm not going to quit trying. I don't know what else to do, but those two are good people. They're worth whatever effort we can make. You have a degree in psychology, Stan. What's your take?"

"Well, I've met Rick and Angie, and they both seem like very nice folks," the new trooper said. "But I don't know anything about their background. What's the real skinny on how they got so messed up?"

"Well, it's complicated," Rob said. "Rick and Angie have been married for nine years or so. He was an all-state high school athlete, and she was a cute cheerleader. It was a storybook romance. His family has always been in the horse business—he had some of the finest Arabians around. They had a great little son. He was a bright kid and almost eight years old when a tragic accident took him. Then all the wheels started to come off.

"It was just before Christmas," he continued. "She went into town to do some shopping and left the boy with his dad for the afternoon. Rick looked out the window and saw a pickup tearing around wildly on his place and went to check it out. He was in a hurry, and he put his son and their dog in the truck and took off. They were clear out on the west end of Rick's ranch on a muddy road when Rick came up over a rise and the pickup T-boned them on the passenger side. It was a cowboy who was just coming from a party in town. The numbers show he was doing about sixty at impact. It was terrible. The boy and the dog never knew what hit 'em. Rick walked away with only minor physical injuries, but it did a number on him mentally.

"The bottom line is that he blames himself. He's on a huge guilt trip because he didn't belt the kid in. Angie was hysterical and said a few things she didn't mean," the trooper continued. "She cried for weeks, and she was upset that Rick never shed a tear. He kept it all bottled up—he still does. Now she feels terrible about what she said, but he thinks she still blames him. It's a mess. She's come around pretty well, but he's an emotional wreck to this day.

"The drunk got off after a year in jail, and Rick went bonkers. I've never seen anger run that deep in a man. He vowed he was going to make the country safe from law breakers like that drunk. He got into the police academy and graduated in the top ten percent. Then he got himself elected county sheriff, and he's been one committed dude.

"The upshot is that he has a demanding job, and he feels more comfortable doing it than going home. He throws himself into it, and she's left to her own resources. He sold his horses, and he vows he'll never have any more kids or own any more dogs.

"It's been almost three years now, and their

relationship is in a free fall. What do you think?" he asked.

"Grief causes some strange behavior," the new trooper said. "What they're experiencing is nothing new. Do you know if they've tried professional counseling?" he asked.

"There's no way," Rob said. "This is a small, tight-knit community, and they're both proud people. Counseling is out of the question."

"That's really too bad," Stan said. "He's got it bottled up, all right, and he's got to get it out so they can deal with it. The problem is that he can't do it alone. They need some outside help. Sounds like Christmas will just make things worse."

"Yeah, no kidding," Rob agreed. "All it is to them is a constant reminder, plus more holiday-related work for him, which means even more loneliness for her. It's a mess. We've all tried, but I'm afraid it's going to take a miracle now."

CHAPTER THREE

As it turned out, Duncan really did have to "go bad," but it was his fascination with the motion-sensing towel dispenser that caused him to take longer than he realized. He didn't even think about how much time had passed, but when he finally emerged from the restroom into an empty convenience store, his heart suddenly leaped into action as he looked through the big window and saw the *Greyhound* moving out.

He didn't have time to think. He wrapped his blanket around himself, grabbed his chips and cup of soda, and ran out the door.

"Wait," he yelled as loudly as he could. "I'm coming! Wait for me! Don't leave me!" But the *Greyhound* showed no sign that anyone inside had seen or heard him. It continued to lumber toward the freeway from which it had come.

Duncan could see no alternative but to catch up

with it. He bolted into a desperate sprint, running faster than he ever thought he could.

Inside the *Greyhound*, Courtney called out urgently. "Dad, stop for a minute! We have a disaster! Danny spilled his drink, and it's dripping on my head."

Burt and Sally exchanged knowing glances, and Burt brought the large van to a stop just before entering the freeway on-ramp. Sally sighed and grabbed the roll of paper towels she usually kept at her feet for such occasions. She unbuckled her seat belt and stepped through the narrow passageway to help with the "disaster." She cleaned up the mess with a few expert wipes, and order was restored.

Outside the lumbering motor home, Duncan felt like his lungs were about to burst. His heart pumped wildly. He wondered how much farther he could go. Then he saw the large, red brake lights come to life and the *Greyhound* come to a stop, and he felt a new surge of energy. His speed slowed, but his volume increased to almost a screech as he lurched onward.

Just as he reached the back bumper, the large unit again began to move. He knew he'd never make it to the door, so he did the only thing he could do. Instinctively, he reached out and grabbed the nearest thing in sight, which happened to be the ladder that led from the bumper up to the roof. A trail of corn chips, soda, and ice spilled out behind him as he spent the last of his energy pulling himself up onto the wide platform that was usually used to carry motorbikes. He panted in exhaustion as the empty paper cup blew out of his hand. The tail pipe belched a cloud of smoke as the *Greyhound* accelerated onto the freeway.

A cold blast of air enveloped Duncan and snatched at whatever remained of his breath. His loose blanket flapped violently, and he almost lost it, but somehow he managed to get a grip on it at the last possible second as the wind swirled around him like a mini-tornado.

Duncan cried out again with everything he had. "Stop! I'm here! Let me in!" He wanted to pound on the side of the motor home, but he didn't dare let go. They had to hear him inside; he couldn't ride all the way to Aunt Millie's like this!

With both hands fiercely gripping the ladder, he tried to hold the blanket against him with his elbows. It didn't work. He could no longer feel his hands. He was freezing. Somehow, he had to get out of this wind. He glanced to his left, and, in the dim glow of the running lights, he saw a small space between the covered spare wheel and the body of the motor home. He made a panic-driven lunge and grabbed fiercely onto the brace on which the wheel was mounted. He wriggled himself into the narrow gap, and for the first time since this adventure began, he felt a small measure of security. In his crouched position, he was finally able to pull his blanket around him, but the cold was still almost unbearable. Whips of wind lashed at his face, and tears streamed down his cheeks.

Man, if I ever get through this, he thought, *I'll never do another stupid thing!*

Even though Duncan's wedged-in position gave him a small refuge, he didn't realize that it also made him practically invisible to any traffic that may approach from behind and to anyone who may be able to alert his parents that he was back there. But under the circumstances, a person cannot think of everything—especially if he's only eight years old! The only thing Duncan could think about was that he had really messed up, and now he just had to hang in there.

Even though his cramped perch was relatively secure and his blanket was pretty snuggly, it was quickly becoming plain that neither was keeping out the fierce cold. His whole body was going numb. His young mind wrestled with the fact that this may very well be his final mess-up. You don't have to be very old to realize when imminent death is a real possibility.

Duncan had always been taught that if you found yourself in a tough spot, you were always supposed to do everything you could possibly do and leave the rest up to Heavenly Father. Why hadn't he thought about that before? He wiped his tears, took advantage of his already bowed head, and uttered the most heartfelt prayer of his young life. He promised Heavenly Father that if he could somehow get out of this pickle, he would never be disobedient again.

Then, immediately after his prayerful plea, almost as he expected it would, the speed of the *Greyhound* began to slow until it came to a complete stop, right in the middle of the freeway.

Up in the cab of the motor home, Burt glanced again at the blue numbers on the digital clock: 2:00 a.m. They hadn't traveled thirty minutes from the Dogwood Creek Café and Truck Stop when, as Burt refocused on the highway, he noticed something oddly out of place in the darkness ahead. They had just passed an exit to a familiar rest stop they had visited on other trips, and at the distant edge of the brightness of the headlights, he thought he saw something moving in front of them. He instinctively lifted his foot from the accelerator and blinked his eyes to make sure he wasn't imagining things. Then he saw it again.

He simultaneously glanced in the rearview mirror to make sure there was no traffic behind them, and pressed his foot to the brake pedal. The big vehicle gradually slowed to a stop.

Sally gasped as she saw it too. There, emerging from the darkness at the edge of the freeway, was a fairly sizeable herd of deer. There must have been twenty or thirty of the graceful animals in various sizes.

"Look at that," she said in disbelief. "How did they ever get past the fence?"

"It looks like somebody's put a hole in it somewhere down there," Burt said. They both watched in fascination as the deer ambled past and almost seemed to surround them. The deer were apparently in no hurry to get anywhere. The antlers of the bucks glistened in the headlights.

"Well, that's something you don't see every day," Burt observed. "I'm glad we saw them in time. That was cool, but it could have been very bad—both for them and for us."

The deer gradually vanished into the darkness on the other side of the freeway, the same way they had appeared. Still shaking his head in amazement, Burt lifted his foot from the brake pedal and again accelerated toward their destination.

CHAPTER FOUR

BACK ON HIS COLD, NARROW perch, Duncan realized in only a few seconds that his prayer had been answered. His somber attitude changed immediately.

"I'm saved!" he yelled, as he excitedly wriggled free from his cramped position behind the spare wheel and jumped awkwardly from the bumper platform to the pavement. His legs were stiff, and he couldn't feel his feet. He stumbled around the corner of the large vehicle and stopped still in amazement. There were deer all over the place! A whole bunch of them.

"Wow! Look at that," Duncan said with unquestioning faith. "Heavenly Father gave me a miracle! He sent reindeer to rescue me!"

It seemed to Duncan that each deer looked at him reassuringly as it passed to let him know that he would be safe.

Duncan felt in his legs and feet the strange tingling feeling that happens when the blood begins to circulate again. His legs felt funny as he awkwardly ran toward the door, fully expecting it to open and let him in. But it didn't. Just like it had before, the motor home again lurched forward and left him watching the running lights melt into the darkness ahead.

"Oh, no! Not again!" he yelled. He bolted forward, but he realized it was no use. Tears welled up in his eyes, and he choked back a sob. Loneliness descended on him like a dark fog.

He could hear rustling and twigs breaking in the darkness where the deer had gone, and somehow it settled him. Although he had no idea what to do next, there was no question in his mind that the deer had been there for him.

When he looked in the direction of the rustling, he was surprised to see a dim, blue light glowing in the darkness and an exit ramp heading off the freeway toward it. He couldn't just stand here in the middle of the freeway, so he drew his blanket around himself and walked toward the glow.

Snowflakes were beginning to fall. They tingled when they touched his nose and cheeks. He instinctively knew he would have to find some shelter pretty soon, but he didn't really worry about it. He was sure that the reindeer and Heavenly Father would take care of him.

When he arrived at the light, he was a little relieved to see that he was in a roadside rest stop and that the light was coming from a telephone booth. He didn't have any money, but that was okay because he really didn't know how to use a pay phone anyway.

Then it dawned on him that the telephone was attached to a small building. In the dim, blue light, he could just barely make out the sign on the door to his left: Men. It was a restroom. He pushed on the door, and it opened.

"All right!" he exclaimed.

It was so dark that he couldn't see anything when he stepped inside. But at least he was out of the snow, and it was much warmer in there than it was outside. He wrapped his blanket around himself, and this time, he could actually feel its warmth and comfort. Tears flowed as he sat down on the floor, leaned his back against the wall, and waited in the darkness.

For the first time in all of this, Duncan thought about his mom and dad and about how worried they would be when they found out he wasn't with them. He felt awfully sorry for his dumb mistake, and he missed them terribly. He prayed that Heavenly Father would take care of them too. With the comforting sound of his reindeer in the trees outside, Duncan fell asleep.

Chapter Five

LIKE A MIST SLOWLY LIFTING, Duncan was aroused from an exhaustion-induced sleep by the rumble of a big motor, the squeaking hiss of large hydraulic equipment, and scraping sounds that made the floor vibrate under him. Faint daylight leaked through the windows, and a few seconds passed before he remembered where he was.

He tried to stand up, but everything hurt. The exertion and the unmoved slumber on the hard floor had taken their toll. He stumbled to the dimly outlined door and had to push hard to get it open. When he did, he gasped in surprise when the light of the early dawn revealed that he was pushing against light, fluffy snow that came almost up to his knees.

"Wow!" he exclaimed, as he saw that it had really snowed during the night and that it was still coming down hard.

When he peered around the door, the sight he saw next caused his heart to do an acrobatic number inside his chest. His eyes widened in surprise as several yards away, a large, orange truck with flashing yellow lights and a huge snowplow on the front was coming right toward him across the trackless parking lot. Deep snow rolled to the side in a huge curl as the truck came closer. When the brightness of the headlights hit his eyes, Duncan jumped up and down and yelled, waving his arms wildly.

The driver saw Duncan and brought the truck to an immediate halt. The door flew open, and the driver jumped out. First he just stared. Then he slowly walked toward what he couldn't believe he was seeing. Even in the gray light, the man looked like he was staring at a ghost.

"Well I'll be ding-danged!" the driver said. "It's a boy! What in the . . ." the man stammered. "Where did *you* come from? Who *are* you?"

Duncan didn't answer; he just screamed in delight and bolted through the one-foot-deep snow toward the awesome-looking form and jumped. The man caught him in mid-air and held on. Duncan's arms flew about the man's neck.

"Man, you'll freeze out here, kid!" the driver said. He unzipped his big, warm parka and pulled the boy in and held him close. Duncan couldn't speak. He just reveled in the wonderful warmth.

Finally, Duncan pushed his face away from the

man's to look him directly in the eyes. "Boy, am I ever glad to see you!" he yelled.

"Well, the same to you, my friend," the surprised man shouted back. "My name's Frank; what's yours?"

"I'm Duncan!" The boy sounded very relieved.

As the big truck idled reassuringly, with its yellow blinking lights dancing off the cascade of snowflakes, Duncan wove the unbelievable, yet undeniable yarn for Frank. He spoke so rapidly, jumping from point to point in the complicated narrative, that Frank had to ask him repeatedly to slow down. When the story finally concluded with the "reindeer" and the night in the restroom, Frank was left with more questions than answers. When he finally thought he understood what he was hearing, he said, "Hold on, Duncan; I gotta phone this in."

Frank picked up the microphone from its clip on the big dashboard and clicked the button. "Dispatch, this is Frank. I have a situation here that I think the Highway Patrol needs to hear. Can you patch me through to Rob Haskell?"

"Sure thing, Frank," a female voice responded. "Hang on a minute." After a moment, the voice came back, "I've got him, Frank. Go ahead."

"You there, Rob?" Frank asked.

"Go ahead, my friend," the trooper replied.

"Fasten your seat belt, partner, 'cause I'm not sure you're gonna believe what I'm gonna tell you."

"Try me, Frank. You have my undivided attention," the trooper smiled.

"Well, I'm sitting in the cab of my truck at the Cedar Springs rest stop with an eight-year-old boy, dressed in pajamas and slippers, who's just spent the night in the restroom. He says he and his family were at the Dogwood, and his folks were going to drive away without him, but he jumped on the back of their motor home and rode clear out here. Then he says some reindeer stopped the motor home, and he jumped off, just as his folks drove on down the road. That was probably five or six hours ago. He's sure they don't know he's not inside with them. What should I do?"

"Frank, does that boy's name happen to be Duncan Watkins?" The trooper suddenly sounded excited.

"Affirmative, Rob! How did you know that?"

"Well, I just talked with two very distraught parents who are going to be very relieved to know you have him. They just pulled into a relative's home up in Carver City and discovered that their eight-year-old boy, Duncan, wasn't with them. They said they'd last seen him at Dogwood, and they have no idea what happened from there. We called Dogwood, and they hadn't seen any lost boys, so I figured that's who you had!"

"Carver City!" Frank exclaimed. "Man, that's three hundred miles from here! How are we gonna get 'em back together?"

"I'll let them know we have him, and we'll work that out later. In the meantime, can you keep him with you until I can get up there? I'm near Dogwood now, so it won't take too long."

"Sure, I can keep him. It will be my pleasure. But the snow's really coming hard, and I'm not sure your cruiser can make it up here. I'm afraid we're gonna have to shut 'er down for a few hours until we can get a handle on it. How 'bout if you wait at Dogwood, and I plow my way down to you? Then I can hand the boy off and break a trail for you back to Millville."

"That sounds good to me, Frank. By the way, we just got a call from division. They're already turning back all southbound traffic at the bottom of Skyline Pass, and northbound traffic at Brush Valley. Do you have an estimate of how long I should tell Duncan's folks it will be before we can get them together?"

"That depends on the storm," Frank responded. "We've never been down for more than twenty-four hours, but from the way it looks now, I'll bet it's at least twelve."

"Ten-four, good buddy," the trooper concluded. "I'll see you at Dogwood."

"Did you hear that, Duncan?" Frank grinned. "Trooper Haskell is gonna tell your folks that we have you and that you're all right."

"That's great," Duncan smiled. "That's real good!"

CHAPTER SIX

THE HANDS ON THE OLD Regulator wall clock in the county sheriff's office stood at 7:05 a.m. Sheriff Rick Bennett stood gazing at the unbelievable snowfall that was in progress outside his window. The cell phone on his belt buzzed into action. When he answered, he was surprised to hear the voice of his friend Trooper Rob Haskell.

"Isn't it kind of early for you to be up and going?" he quipped.

"No earlier than it is for you," came the trooper's response. "They say there's no rest for the wicked—or the lawman. Rick, I'm on my way over to your place from Dogwood. I have the boy Frank found up at Cedar Springs. The weather is complicating things, so I guess I need your help. I called your place, and Angie said you were already at the office. She gave me your cell phone number."

"Good! I've been tracking that, and I'm glad you're bringing him in. How can we help?"

"Well, I've contacted his parents and don't know whether they're more grateful or embarrassed. His dad said he was turning right around and coming back to get his boy. I told him we were working on a way to get him here, but it's looking pretty bleak. I asked him to give me a few minutes to work something out and get back to him. Everything's shut down for at least twelve hours and maybe more. I think we're going to have to keep him overnight. Can we get the county's family emergency services involved?"

"I expected as much when I got the word that he'd been found," Rick said, "and I've already talked with Melba Matthews over in Crescent this morning. She's very willing to do whatever she can, but there are four-foot-deep show drifts on the road between here and there, and it's going to be a while before anybody can get through."

"I know what you mean," Rob said. "As we speak, I'm following Frank's snowplow. If I weren't, I'd be in trouble."

"We could probably get him over there," the sheriff said, "But his folks couldn't get there as quickly as they could get here."

"Well, I could take him home with me," Trooper Haskell said, "unless you have any better ideas."

There was a significant pause on the other end. The sheriff seemed to be in deep thought.

"No, you have your family to look after," he finally said. "Knowing you guys, you could probably work him in just fine, but I've been thinking about it since I got the word, and it wouldn't be any trouble for Angie and me to keep the boy at our place until his folks can come and get him. That would have the least impact on everyone for Christmas Eve. We have plenty of room, and she certainly has the time."

Now there was a long, knowing pause as the trooper processed that offer.

"Rick, are you sure about this?" he finally asked, with a tone that was a blend of surprise and concern.

"Yes, I am," Rick responded.

"How will Angie feel about it?" the trooper asked.

"I'm pretty sure she'll be willing, but we can find out in a minute. Hang on; I'll get her on the line."

The short story is that Angie didn't hesitate to agree for even a second. Duncan said it was fine with him, and a quick call to George Abbott—the local Justice of the Peace for his judicial sanction—sealed the deal.

Burt and Sally Watkins weren't thrilled that they would have to share their son with someone else for Christmas Eve, but under the circumstances, they didn't have any other option. The main thing was that Duncan was safe and sound and in good hands, and they were tremendously relieved and grateful.

Chapter Seven

Well, look at you, you brave little guy!" Angie said as Rick and Duncan walked in the door of their rustic ranch home. "You must be ready for a good breakfast and a warm bath, right? And your pajamas and blanket look like they've really . . ." she searched for the right words, "come in handy!"

"That would be awesome!" Duncan smiled.

Now, Duncan was not the kind of kid who liked to soak endlessly in the tub, but this bath was a remarkable exception. The warm water surrounded him and seemed to soak into him. It was as if all of the trials of his long night were being washed away, one by one. He felt like he could just stay there forever.

Never had there been a breakfast like the one that followed the bath. Duncan and Angie were a good team. She loved to cook, and he loved to eat. And they both gave their personal-best performances.

Angie put Duncan's pajamas, slippers, and blanket in the washer and dressed him temporarily in one of Sheriff Rick's T-shirts, tied with a brown ribbon around his middle.

"We'll have to find something more permanent," she said, "but are you okay with that for a little while?" With the tied, oversized T-shirt and his bare feet, he said he felt like a sumo wrestler.

Sheriff Rick had to get back to work, but he promised he'd be home as soon as possible. After that soothing bath and with all that good food in him, Duncan began to feel the effect of his stress and lack of restful sleep the night before. His face stretched into a wide yawn. Angie brought out a big, soft pillow and a snuggly blanket, and within minutes, Duncan was sound asleep on the big, leather couch.

When he woke up, Angie was sitting in the wooden rocking chair, watching him. She wiped tears from her cheeks but smiled and winked a greeting at him.

"I have some Christmas presents for you, Duncan," she said softly. She reached down and picked up three colorful packages, each sporting big, red ribbons.

"Wow!" Duncan's eyes widened. "Where did you get Christmas presents?"

"Well," she carefully began. "I actually bought them for Christmas three years ago. We used to have a son who was about your age. I bought them for him. Then, before I could give them to him, he was suddenly taken away. I have kept them all this time. I couldn't bear to give them up. It seemed like they kept him closer to me.

"But I've been thinking about it. You need clothes, and I happen to have some—and I want you to have them. Are you okay with that?"

She was weeping now, and Duncan felt tears running down his own cheeks too. He could tell that her feelings were very important to her. His tender heart reached out, and his young mind searched for something to say that wouldn't sound stupid. But all he could think of was, "Thanks for being so good to me."

The new clothes fit Duncan perfectly. The phone rang, and Angie answered it and talked briefly. After she hung up, she smiled.

"Well, this is quite a day, Duncan," she said. "Sheriff Rick usually doesn't come home until very late. We rarely have dinner together. But he just called and said he'd be home around five o'clock. He wondered if the three of us could have a Christmas Eve dinner together. Would that be all right with you?"

"Oh, yes," Duncan said enthusiastically. "Sheriff Rick has been very nice to me when I really don't deserve it," he said, lowering his voice. "I'm only here because I really messed up. Someone asked me why I didn't just go back into the store and have the clerk call the Highway Patrol. I guess I should have. I sure could have saved everybody a lot of trouble, but I didn't think about it," he continued. "I knew I needed to do everything I could, and I just did what I thought was best. But Sheriff Rick didn't even ask. He just likes me anyway."

"Duncan, cut yourself a little slack," Angie said, taking his hand like mothers do. "You're eight! You wanted to be with your family. You didn't mess up. You did a very brave thing. Of course Sheriff Rick likes you, and so do I. We always have to choose if we'll follow our hearts or our heads, and right now, your head is just jealous that this time, you followed your heart."

"Thanks," Duncan said. "I hope my mom and dad feel the same way."

"Of course they do, silly; they're your mom and dad! They will be so glad to get you back. There will be a big celebration when you get home; you wait and see."

"Sheriff Rick looks at you the way my dad looks at my mom," Duncan said.

Angie was clearly surprised. "Is that good?" she asked warily.

"It's the best!" Duncan said. "My dad really loves my mom."

Again, tears pooled in Angie's eyes. "You don't miss much, do you, kid?" she said as she playfully poked him on the shoulder.

Several silent moments passed.

"Will you tell me about your son?" Duncan finally asked. "What was his name, and what happened to him?"

Angie was willing to talk about it, but she wasn't sure how to begin. She drew a breath and struggled to control her voice. She spoke slowly and carefully, "His name was Ricky, after his father. He was so cute and smart. In fact, he was a lot like you. One day when he was almost eight, just before Christmas, he got in the truck with his daddy and his dog to go chase a wild man who was tearing up our place." Tears welled up and she paused to maintain control. "They were in such a hurry that he didn't buckle up. When they found the man, he ran into them with his truck, and Ricky and his dog were killed."

She needed to pause again. "Ever since, Sheriff Rick hasn't liked himself very much because he didn't fasten the seat belt. And because of some dumb things I said at the time, he thinks I don't like him either— but I do. I love him very much. Besides, I don't know if the seat belt would have made any difference anyway," she sniffled. "He said he would never have any more kids or own any more dogs.

"The wild man got off easy," she continued, "and that made Sheriff Rick want to become a lawman. He did, and he's very good at it. He works very hard to help make sure that kind of thing doesn't happen anymore."

Angie's face brightened as Sheriff Rick's truck pulled into the driveway at three thirty. He said he couldn't keep his mind on his work, so he thought he'd better come home where he could be more useful.

"Wow! You look great, kiddo!" he said, noticing Duncan's new outfit. "Where did you get the new duds?"

"Come here for a minute," Angie motioned to her husband. "You and I need a brief, private conference. Will you excuse us, Duncan?"

They left the room for a few minutes, and when they came back, they were arm in arm. Angie was dabbing at tears again, but they were both smiling.

"Have a seat," Sheriff Rick said to Duncan as he motioned to the big, overstuffed chair.

"We talked with your folks a while ago," the sheriff said, "And they've agreed that we can keep you overnight and fly you up to Carver City tomorrow on a helicopter. Does that sound cool? The weather should be good enough by then. That will have the least impact on your family and their holiday plans."

"Wow! You mean I get to ride in a real helicopter? That would be awesome!" Duncan grinned. "Are my parents okay? I mean, are they mad or anything?"

"Your parents are fine," the sheriff said. "They're really good people. They'll be so glad to get you back. How could they ever be mad at you? You're a hero."

"What did I tell you?" Angie smiled.

"Your mom wanted to talk with you on the phone," the sheriff continued. "I told her we'd call as soon as I got home. Is that good?"

"Yes, that's cool!" Duncan said excitedly.

The phone call was brief, but it did everything that was needed to assure a worried mom that her little boy was warm, safe, and happy and was going to be looked after properly on Christmas Eve.

After the phone call, Duncan looked around the room and asked, "Where's your Christmas tree? It's Christmas Eve. How come you don't have a tree?"

"Well, that's a long story," Sheriff Rick said, "but I guess a tree would really brighten up the place, wouldn't it? How 'bout if after dinner, you and I snowshoe up the hill and cut one?"

"Awesome! I've never done that before!" Duncan smiled, raising both thumbs in the air with approval.

CHAPTER EIGHT

DUNCAN AND SHERIFF RICK BOTH agreed that
the Christmas Eve dinner Angie prepared was, indeed,
awesome, and the snowshoe trip up the hill through
knee-deep snow left Duncan breathless in more ways
than one. Angie found some Christmas decorations
that hadn't been disturbed for more than three years,
and after an hour or so, the Bennett home was a cheery
Christmas scene. The Bennetts and their eight-year-
old guest—with their newly decorated Christmas tree
looking on—sang silly songs, ate goodies until they
were stuffed, and finally ran out of energy.

"It's been a great party," Sheriff Rick finally said,
"but I think it's about bedtime."

"In my family," Duncan said, "we always read the
Christmas story from the Bible. Could we do that
before we go to bed?"

"I haven't read that story for so long. I wouldn't

even know where to find it," the sheriff said.

"Well, I know where it is," Angie interrupted with a teasing tone. "I haven't forgotten. I know the exact place."

She went to a drawer in a large cabinet and took out a big, worn bible. They sat in a small circle on the floor, and she quickly found the place in the book of Luke. She handed it to her husband to read. He gave her a very troubled look, but he took it and made a start: "And it came to pass in those days, that there went out a decree from Cæsar Augustus, that all the world should be taxed . . ." Suddenly, his voice choked, and tears pooled in his eyes. He tried to go on, but only stifled sobbing sounds came out. Angie's eyes widened. She touched his arm with concern, and he wept openly as he handed the book to her. Then she wiped her eyes too and continued to read:

"And Joseph also went up out of the city of Nazareth, into Judea, unto the city of David, which is called Bethlehem . . ."

By the time she finished the story, everyone was sniffling warm, soothing, healing tears.

"Boy, what an experience," Sheriff Rick said. "That's been a long time coming. I guess we all needed that in our own way."

The little Christmas tree twinkled happily as the little circle of family sat in a big group hug and wept together for a longer time than any of them realized.

Finally, Duncan was tucked into a comfortable

bed in a room that was obviously decorated for a little boy. He asked if they could say prayers together, and again the three of them knelt on the floor in a circle. Duncan's prayer was a simple thanks for his family, for Angie and Sheriff Rick, for Frank and the reindeer, and for everyone who had helped him that day. He prayed that they would all be blessed, and there was no question in his mind that they would be, indeed.

CHAPTER NINE

ANGIE, I'VE BEEN A REAL JERK," Rick said as they walked back to the living room, arm in arm. "I've been so angry that I focused on getting even to the exclusion of almost everything else. Somehow, I needed that little kid to come into my life and help me get things sorted out. When they brought him in off that mountain and we needed a place for him to stay, I can't describe how strongly I felt that we should take him in. Thanks for backing me up. It was like he'd been sent to us. For me, it was nothing short of a miracle."

"I know the feeling," Angie said. "Before you got home, he told me what a great guy you are and how good you've been to him. I didn't disagree with him one bit. It was very wrong for me to spout untrue and cruel things at you in the middle of my hysteria. I'm so sorry, Rick."

Rick and Angie truly embraced for the first time since the tragedy.

"It's been really nice to have a little kid around again," Angie said, "and a husband too, as a matter of fact! I've felt things that I haven't felt for three years."

They wept together and held each other for a long time.

"I know it won't be easy," Rick finally said, "but do you think you can ever forgive me? Do you think we can put things back together again?"

"There was never anything to forgive," she said, looking straight into his eyes. "I worked that out a long time ago, and I have prayed ever since that you would too."

In the little bedroom down the hallway, Duncan smiled contentedly as he drifted off to sleep in the soft, warm covers—and he never even had one thought about Bagley Bear.

Chapter Ten

By morning, the storm had passed, and the sun was shining brightly. A small crowd had gathered at the helicopter pad to see them off. Frank was there, and so was Maggie, the dispatcher. Troopers Rob and Stan came too. Duncan thought Angie glowed like a real angel. She couldn't keep from grinning, and her eyes twinkled the whole time through little pools of happy tears.

As Duncan and Sheriff Rick climbed aboard the helicopter, Angie wanted one last hug. And that started a hug epidemic that went clear around the circle of well-wishers.

Even though Duncan couldn't wait to get to Aunt Millie's, the ride to Carver City was over almost too soon. And speaking of hugs, when Duncan ran from the helicopter into the arms of his waiting family, there was a major group hug that went on and on. The tears—even from his siblings—just seemed to keep coming.

When Sheriff Rick finally stepped into the crowd to say good-bye, Burt and Sally asked him if he wouldn't stay for dinner.

"I'd love to," he said, "but I gotta get back. I have a date with my sweetheart. We're going to ride out to see a friend of ours who breeds dogs. We called him this morning, and he has a Boarder Collie puppy he thinks we'll like." He smiled and winked at Duncan's wide-eyed grin and got an enthusiastic thumbs-up in return.

"Now you keep in touch, Duncan," Sheriff Rick said. "You hold some major stock in our family, and you and your folks are welcome at our place anytime."

Chapter Eleven

Finally, Duncan was alone with his mom and dad in the back seat of Aunt Millie's car. They couldn't keep their hands off of him. As he sat between them, his dad said, "Duncan, do you realize that you have personally experienced a series of real-life Christmas miracles?"

"Yes, I do, Dad. I did everything I could; I prayed hard, and Heavenly Father took care of me," he said sincerely.

"Well, we have a ton of questions to ask you about what really happened out there, but we want you to know they can wait until you feel like sharing."

"Thanks, Dad," Duncan said. "But right now, I just want to know one thing. Am I gonna be grounded for life for this?"

"Are you kidding?" both parents exclaimed at once. "No way! You're a hero!"

"Whew!" Duncan exclaimed in exaggerated relief. "Then that's the best Christmas miracle of all!"

About the Authors

TED AND SHIRLENE HINDMARSH have loved each other for almost fifty years. They are distinctly different people, but they readily acknowledge that when they work as a team, those differences are strengthening and result in a product that is better than either of them could have produced alone. So they team up on everything important—parenting, church assignments, gardening, remodeling, and, with this little project, writing a story.

They also love Christmas and all its tenderness and tradition. For more than thirty years, Ted has written an original Christmas story or verse each year for his loved ones. Three of those stories—*Cracked Wheat for Christmas, The Coachmen and the Bells,* and *Who Was Jolly Holiday?*—have found their way to publication.

Ted recently retired from forty-four years of service at Brigham Young University, where he worked as an administrator with educational media, learning resource centers, the Freshman Academy, and the honor code office. He is also a journalist, and he taught as an adjunctive faculty member in the communications department.

Shirlene focused on her job as a wife and mother until all of her five children were in school. Then she began her professional career as an academic advisor at BYU. She recently retired as the supervisor of the advisement center for the College of Health and Human Performance, where she has enjoyed serving students for twenty-five years.

Ted and Shirlene have two daughters, three sons, eighteen grandchildren, and four great-grandchildren.